# The
# SNOW LION

For Karen and Nina – JH

For Phoebe and Kitty – RJ

**SIMON & SCHUSTER**
First published in Great Britain in 2017 by Simon and Schuster UK Ltd,
1st Floor, 222 Gray's Inn Road, London WC1X 8HB • A CBS Company
Text copyright © 2017 Jim Helmore • Illustrations copyright © 2017
Richard Jones • The right of Jim Helmore and Richard Jones to be identified
as the author and illustrator of this work has been asserted by them in
accordance with the Copyright, Designs and Patents Act, 1988 • All rights
reserved, including the right of reproduction in whole or in part in any
form • A CIP catalogue record for this book is available from the British
Library upon request • Printed in Italy • ISBN: 978-1-4711-6223-7 (HB)
ISBN: 978-1-4711-6224-4 (PB) • ISBN: 978-1-4711 6225-1 (eBook)
10 9 8 7 6 5 4 3 2 1

# The
# SNOW LION

## Jim Helmore and Richard Jones

**SIMON & SCHUSTER**
London   New York   Sydney   Toronto   New Delhi

Caro and her mum went to live
in a new house at the top of a hill.

The walls were white, the ceilings were white,

even the doors were white.

There were lots of places for Caro to explore.
But she wished she had someone to play with.

Then, one day, she heard a noise.

'How about a game of hide-and-seek?'
said a deep, gentle voice.

Caro turned around.

There stood a lion, as white as snow.
'Where did you come from?' Caro asked.

'Oh, here and there,'
said the lion.

He leant against the white wall and vanished.
The wall winked at her and Caro laughed.

They played hide-and-seek . . .

. . . all day.

The next morning, Caro and the lion looked
out of the window and saw two boys.
Their colourful kites swooped and soared.

One of the boys waved, but Caro shyly looked away.

'Come on, let's play again!' she said.

All week, the lion and Caro climbed and slid.

They raced

and they chased.

Then, one day, the lion looked thoughtful.

'Have you tried the slide in the park?' he asked.
'I like playing here with you,' said Caro.

'I'll still be here when you get back,'
the lion replied.

So Caro went to the park.

When she got there, she found the boy who
had waved at her yesterday. The boy's name was
Bobby and he could slide almost as well as the lion.

'Can't catch me!' laughed Bobby,
but by now Caro was very good at chasing.

'How was the slide?' asked the lion, that night.
'Bumpy!' smiled Caro. 'But I missed you.'

The next day, Bobby asked Caro if she'd like to play with his friends.

'Give it a try,' said the lion.
'But I won't know anyone,' she whispered.
'You'll have a great time,' said the lion,
'and you do know Bobby.'

So Caro went to Bobby's house,
where they all built a Pirate Spaceship Kitchen.

After they had reached the moon they buried
their treasure and ate plenty of chocolate cake.

The next morning, Caro's mum said, 'I think it's time
we put some colour into this house, don't you?'

'I like it white,' said Caro, uncertainly.

Just then, the doorbell rang.

Her mum had invited all Caro's new friends for a painting party!

Soon the house was full of oranges, reds, blues and greens, and by the afternoon everyone needed a bath.

That night Caro searched everywhere for the lion,
but there were no white walls or white ceilings or
white doors left.

Outside it began to snow. Soon the whole hill was white.
Down in the garden, something caught Caro's eye.

Could it be?

'I thought I'd never see you again!' cried Caro.

'All lions are happiest outdoors,' said the lion,
'and you've got other friends to play with now.'

'But I'll miss you.'

The lion smiled. 'And I'll miss you too.
But if you need me, you'll know where to look.'

And she did.